SPARKY AND EDDIE
WILD, WILD RODEO!

by **Tony Johnston**
pictures by **Susannah Ryan**

HELLO READER! — LEVEL 3

SCHOLASTIC INC. **Cartwheel** ·B·O·O·K·S·®
New York Toronto London Auckland Sydney

A NOTE TO PARENTS

Reading Aloud with Your Child

Research shows that reading books aloud is the single most valuable support parents can provide in helping children learn to read.

- Be a ham! The more enthusiasm you display, the more your child will enjoy the book.
- Run your finger underneath the words as you read to signal that the print carries the story.
- Leave time for examining the illustrations more closely; encourage your child to find things in the pictures.
- Invite your youngster to join in whenever there's a repeated phrase in the text.
- Link up events in the book with similar events in your child's life.
- If your child asks a question, stop and answer it. The book can be a means to learning more about your child's thoughts.

Listening to Your Child Read Aloud

The support of your attention and praise is absolutely crucial to your child's continuing efforts to learn to read.

- If your child is learning to read and asks for a word, give it immediately so that the meaning of the story is not interrupted. DO NOT ask your child to sound out the word.
- On the other hand, if your child initiates the act of sounding out, don't intervene.
- If your child is reading along and makes what is called a miscue, listen for the sense of the miscue. If the word "road" is substituted for the word "street," for instance, no meaning is lost. Don't stop the reading for a correction.
- If the miscue makes no sense (for example, "horse" for "house"), ask your child to reread the sentence because you're not sure you understand what's just been read.
- Above all else, enjoy your child's growing command of print and make sure you give lots of praise. *You are your child's first teacher — and the most important one. Praise from you is critical for further risk-taking and learning.*

— Priscilla Lynch
Ph.D., New York University
Educational Consultant

Text copyright © 1998 by Roger D. Johnston and Susan T. Johnston,
as trustees of the Johnston Family Trust.
Illustrations copyright © 1998 by Susannah Ryan.
All rights reserved. Published by Scholastic Inc.
HELLO READER! and CARTWHEEL BOOKS and associated logos
are trademarks and/or registered trademarks of Scholastic Inc.
A hardcover edition of *Sparky and Eddie: Wild, Wild Rodeo!*
is being published simultaneously by Scholastic Press.

Library of Congress Cataloging-in-Publication Data

Johnston, Tony, 1942 –
        Sparky and Eddie : wild, wild rodeo / by Tony Johnston ; pictures by
Susannah Ryan
        p.   cm.— (Hello reader! Level 3)
        "Cartwheel Books."
        Summary: When two best friends compete in a mock rodeo at school,
they learn that winning is not everything.
        ISBN 0-590-47985-7
        [1. Schools — Fiction. 2. Friendship — Fiction.
3. Cowboys — Fiction.] I. Ryan, Susannah, ill. II. Title.
        PZ7.J6478Sp   1997
[E] — dc20   96-38188
                                                                   CIP
                                                                    AC
10 9 8 7 6 5 4 3   8 9/9 0/0 01 02

Printed in the U.S.A.   24
First Cartwheel printing, April 1998

For Gayle and Gary Libberton
and for the kids of Black Bob School,
Olathe, Kansas — YA-HOO!
— T. J.

For Polly, our cowgirl.
— S. R.

Sparky and Eddie were excited.

Today was the rodeo.

It was Sparky's class against Eddie's.

Sparky wore a vest with fringe,
jeans, a string tie,
and his father's boots.
The boots were too big.
He could hardly walk.
But he didn't care.
He was a cowboy
and happy.

Eddie wore a shirt with a cow,
jeans, a red bandanna,
and his father's hat.
The hat was too big.
He could hardly see.
But he didn't care.
He was a cowboy and happy.

Sparky and Eddie galloped to school.
They galloped on sock-headed horses.
They smacked their jeans with their hands.
SMACK! SMACK! SMACK!

They carried teddy bears.
"YA-HOO!" they yelled,
all the way to school.

Their classes gathered outside.
All the kids were cowboys.
Or cowgirls.
They all had teddy bears.
They all galloped around on
sock-headed horses.
They all smacked their jeans.
SMACK! SMACK! SMACK!
They all yelled, "YA-HOO!"

BOOT HILL ➡

TEDDY BEAR ROPING ⬅

"Settle down," a teacher said.

He gave them his settle-down look.

Eddie didn't settle down.

He kept galloping.

Sparky wanted the rodeo to start.

He wanted his class to win.

"Settle down," Sparky told Eddie.

He gave Eddie his settle-down look.

Eddie settled down.

The principal said, "Howdy.

Welcome to the rodeo.

We have three events.

The class with the most points wins."

Then she yelled, "YA-HOO!"

The first event was Teddy Bear Roping.

Really, it was stringing.

The kids had to run to their teddy bears,

then tie their bears' legs together

with string.

Kids set their teddy bears down.

Sparky and Eddie did that, too.

The principal called,
"*One, two, three.*
GO!"
The ropers ran to their teddy bears.

They grabbed their teddy bears.
They tossed their teddy bears down.
Then, loop, loop, loop,
they tied some legs together.
They tied fast.

They tied *so* fast,
some kids tied their fingers in
with the teddy bear legs.
Eddie tied his thumb.

Sparky's class won.

They got ten points.

"YA-HOO!" Sparky yelled.

He liked to win.

The Boot Search was next.
Kids pulled off their boots
and threw them in a pile.
The pile was Boot Hill.
Teachers mixed up the boots.
The first class to find theirs
and put them back on would win.

The principal called,
"*One, two, three.*
GO!"

The kids dashed and darted
and dug for their boots.
They screeched and screamed
and scrambled for their boots.
They hooted and scooted
and rooted for their boots.

Sparky's boots were so big,
he found them first.
His whole class found
their boots first.
They got ten points.
"YA-HOO!" yelled Sparky.
He liked to win.

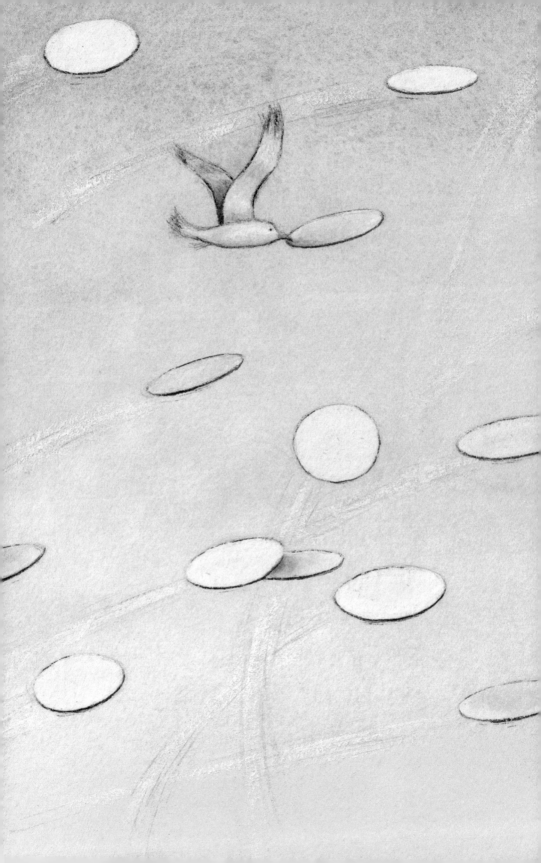

The Tortilla Toss was last.
At a signal,
the teams tossed stale tortillas.
Tortillas and tortillas and tortillas.
They sailed through the air
like thin, white Frisbees.

Sparky's class was ahead.

It was Eddie's turn.

His tortilla was ready.

Eddie was ready.

But—his hat fell over his eyes.

Eddie couldn't see.

He tossed anyway.

His tortilla sailed far.

So far, his class won.

They got twenty points.

"*Pooh!*" Sparky said.

He hated to lose.

Now the points were even.

The classes were tied.

No one had won.

The principal said,

"We'll have one more event.

Whoever names the most uses

for a bandanna wins the rodeo."

"Uses for a *banana*?" the kids asked.

"Bandanna," she said.

Sparky's class huddled.
They knew about bandannas.
They yelled a bandanna list.
Their teacher wrote it—fast.
They yelled things like:

fix broken
bones
cover eyes
cover mouth
wipe sweat

They yelled fifteen things
for their bandanna list.

Eddie's class huddled.

They didn't know about bandannas.

They yelled a bandanna list.

They yelled:

"WE DON'T KNOW!"

Eddie said, "Wait."

Eddie liked to know stuff.

He knew about bandannas.

He yelled a new bandanna list
for his class.

The teacher wrote it—fast.

He yelled things like:

GAG
RAG
BAG
HATBAND
DIAPER
FLAG

Eddie yelled thirty-four things
for the bandanna list.
Eddie's class won the rodeo.
"YA-HOO!" Eddie shouted.
"YA-HOO!" his class shouted.

"POOH!" Sparky shouted.
He was mad.
He was so mad,
he started to cry.
He stomped off.
He stomped off in his too-big boots
to let his tears fall—alone.

Eddie found Sparky.

Eddie felt sad.

"Sorry I knew about bandannas,"
he said.

Sparky looked at Eddie.

"You couldn't help it," Sparky said.

"You're a brain."

Then he said, "Sorry I got mad.

I'm glad you won."

"You are?" Eddie asked.

"Yes. I like you better
than I like to win.

You are my best friend."

Eddie felt happy then.

He looked at Sparky's wet face.

He smiled.

"I know one more use for a bandanna."

"What?" Sparky asked.

"To dry tears."

Eddie gave his bandanna to Sparky.

"Thanks." Sparky smiled.

Then they smacked their jeans.
SMACK! SMACK! SMACK!
And they galloped their sock-headed
horses to their rooms.
"YA-HOO!" they yelled.
For they were cowboys and happy.